BROWNIE BOY

Written By LaTrell Halcomb

Illustrated By Muhammad Isnaeni

Hi, I'm Mike! I am so excited to get out of school and rush home.

My mom makes brownies every Friday! Guess what today is...FRIDAY! I ran onto the bus and told the bus driver to please hurry.

I rushed inside my house and I could smell the delicious chocolatey brownies in the oven.

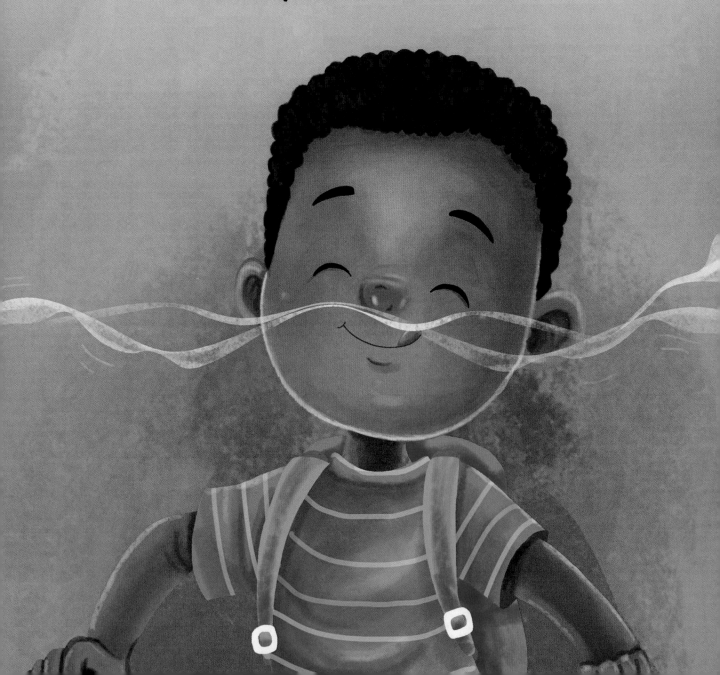

I ran to mom and asked, "Can I please have a brownie?"

Mom replied, "Mike, I'm cooking dinner right now but if you finish all your food later, you may have a brownie."

I frowned, and said, "okay mom" and quietly went to my room.

Dad walked in from work and noticed that I was sad. He cheered me up and asked if I could help him with setting the table for dinner.

When we finished, I hurried and asked mom
"Can I please have a brownie now?"

Mom smirked and shook her head no and said,
"Patience Mike, you need to learn to be patient.
Dinner is almost done."

Mom also suggested that I clean my room while she finished dinner.

I asked "Do I have to?" Mom said, "The faster you clean your room the faster you can eat dinner and eat your favorite brownies!"

I ran quickly out of the kitchen as fast as I could.
I began picking up toys and placed them in the toy
box. Grabbed the clothes off the floor and tossed them
in the basket.

I ran and threw away all the trash in sight, faster than someone could say brownies.

Finally, I'm finished! I shouted out "I'm done Mom." Mom shouted back, "Dinner is done Mike."

All that went through my mind was the chocolatey taste I was going to inhale. I'm getting closer and closer to being able to eat brownies.

I got to the table and didn't waste any time.
I took a couple of bites when suddenly my stomach
started to hurt.

I asked to be excused.

Mom started to worry.

So she rushed to check on me to see if I was ok.

Mom looked all over the house for me and finally went into my room.

She found me asleep with brownie crumbs all over my lap and chocolate all over my face.

Mom smiled from ear to ear and laughed and gave me the biggest kiss and said, "Goodnight, Brownie Boy."

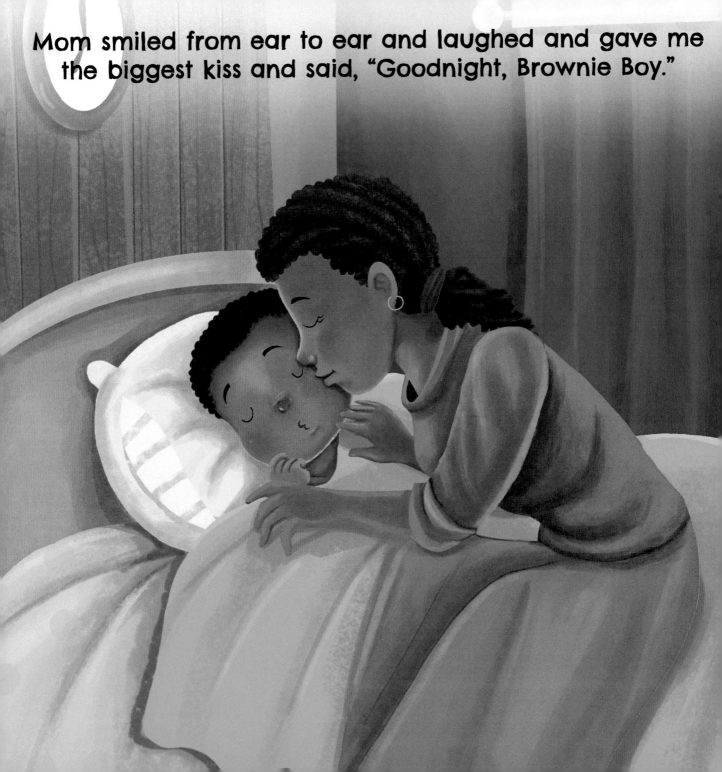

Made in the USA
Middletown, DE
15 October 2023

40378993R00015